DENISOVAN HARMONY

DJ COCKBURN

Published by Water Dragon Publishing
waterdragonpublishing.com

ISBN 978-1-959804-85-7 (Trade Paperback)

FIRST EDITION

10 9 8 7 6 5 4 3 2 1

DENISOVAN HARMONY

THE DENISOVANS were thirteen years old when they sang for the first time.

Tora and I were in the building, watching them on the screens. The six of them trooped through the Ponderosa pines and into a clearing but instead of chasing each other around in one of their games of tag that seemed to have a different set of rules every time, they walked into the middle and knelt in a circle.

It could have been a coincidence that they were in boy-girl-boy order. It could have been intentional. We'd never seen them do anything like this before so we had no clue.

Our view tilted as the AI flew the drone that had been following them out from under the pines and sent it soaring above them, giving us a view from directly above.

"They're naked," said Tora.

I zoomed the image to check. She was right. They'd started taking an interest in the fabric we'd left out for them — making sure they didn't know who was leaving it — a year ago, when they first started showing signs of puberty. It didn't take them long to work out how to tie the fabric into loincloths, demonstrating an adolescent instinct for modesty and adding to the evidence that *Homo denisova* shared the instincts of *Homo sapiens*. The Denisovans were oblivious to the academic paper and three conference presentations they inspired while they entertained themselves with more elaborate ways to tie their cloths, but now they were bare bodied and empty-handed.

That was when they sang.

They opened their mouths together and let out a single note. If one of them sang first, I couldn't have said who. One note arose from six deep chests, rising in volume until it stopped as if cut with an axe.

Then came a higher note. Then a lower note.

"Are they all singing at once or is it two or three at a time?" I asked.

"I don't know." Tora was hearing the song through the same speakers I was. The AI had brought in two more drones to let us watch and listen, but the sound was all piped through one speaker.

The drones showed us three different angles on the kneeling Denisovans and transmitted the song with perfect fidelity, but they couldn't answer my question. I waited for Tora to remind me that we were supposed to stay in the building when the Denisovans showed a new behavior in case we influenced it.

The look on Tora's face said she was waiting for me to remind her. We'd been the only sapiens out here for six weeks, so we'd each got pretty good at knowing what the other was thinking.

The speakers relayed a change in the timbre of the Denisovans' voices. It sounded like the boys had dropped the note by an octave while the girls went higher. They were far enough through puberty for it to make a difference.

A tear ran down Tora's cheek. Our Denisovans were *singing*.

Screw what we weren't supposed to do. We grabbed our jackets and dashed for the door.

I followed Tora, towering over her and struggling to keep up at the same time. Her lithe five-three was much better suited to the Oregon pine forest than I was. I moved like a pro wrestler a few years after exchanging steroids and gym time for burgers and fries. Tora flitted between branches that smacked me in the mouth while I lumbered after her. I really needed to lose thirty pounds and this time I meant it — just like all the other times I'd meant it.

After nearly ten minutes of lumbering through the forest, I heard the Denisovan song over my own panting. I'd almost lost sight of Tora when she stopped and crouched against the light of the clearing. I tried not to puff too much as I joined her, huddled against a trunk that gave us a clear view of them without making us too obvious.

Not that we could have hidden if they'd wanted to find us. They were already sneaking up on white-tailed deer with the spears they'd copied from the ones the project had left for them to examine. They'd got so good at it that the nutrient bars they'd once lived on had become their candy rather than their staple, which had provided the content for two more papers. Or perhaps it was three. I left writing to the Denisovan project's academics.

They could hear an overweight, urbanized sapiens like me long before I knew they were within shouting distance. If they weren't looking at us, it was because they weren't interested in us. They were all staring rigidly ahead, which meant their eyes were fixed on whoever was opposite them.

"How do they *know*?" Tora whispered.

It was a rhetorical question. The first six Denisovans in the world for tens of thousands of years — we still didn't know how many tens of thousands — had never known anyone who could have taught them how to sing.

All six of them merged their voices into a single harmony. I decided I didn't care how they knew. I simply loved them for it. If that wasn't very scientific of me, so what? I wasn't an academic and it had been years since I'd felt this much like a father.

Their heads were starting to turn. I was focusing on Palat, who happened to be the closest to facing me. I took the moment to see how much he'd changed in the last year. Blond fuzz spread from his chin to merge with gold locks on his head tumbling over pale brown skin. His eyebrows crested the brow ridge he'd developed in the last year. The boy was becoming a man.

A man whose head was turning to his left. He was looking at Pilun. They were all looking at Pilun, who sat between Palat and Sabul.

Something on Pilun's face focused my attention on her. It's difficult to read someone's emotions when they're singing. Whatever they're doing with their mouth defines their features, so their expression changes moment by moment. But with five unblinking stares on her, Pilun's eyes were darting around the circle.

The song changed to a set of overlapping notes. Desar started it as a solo, holding his bass monotone for longer than any sapiens could have matched without years of training. As it started to fade, Gavrab came in with her alto. She passed it on to Sabul's tenor, to Beshar's soprano and around the circle until it got to Palat.

As Palat filled the clearing with his own rich bass, I couldn't mistake Pilun's expression. Wide-eyed terror is coded into genes that were ancient when our sapiens ancestors went one way while the Denisovans' went another.

Palat's note began to fade. Pilun opened her mouth, swallowed, tried again and managed a cough.

Palat's note faded to silence.

Pilun took a breath and let out a sound that I could only describe as a squawk. I had to stifle a laugh. Singing is hard work, and this was their first attempt. Someone had to falter first.

Then I saw Pilun wasn't laughing.

Even at thirteen, the Denisovans' bodies were stockier than most adult sapiens. A lot of their bulk was in the thicker bones, but big bones need big muscles to move them and when they want to, Denisovans can move *fast*.

No pubescent sapiens could have matched the speed and grace with which the five of them fell on Pilun.

I hesitated. If this was one of their boisterous games, we weren't supposed to interfere. They'd never seriously hurt each other before.

Palat grabbed a rock and smashed it against Pilun's head.

Tora and I reacted at the same moment, which meant she was three paces ahead of me before I was out of my crouch.

I was so concerned about Pilun that I didn't think to wonder whether Tora and I should be worried about ourselves until Tora was already on them.

All three of the boys outweighed her but she didn't care. She grabbed Palat's wrist and hauled him to his feet with the bloodied stone still in his hand. Screamed in his face. I couldn't make out the words so perhaps she was screaming in Swedish or perhaps she wasn't using words at all, but I couldn't misunderstand her rage and anguish. Neither could Palat, who dropped the stone and backed away.

I caught up and grabbed the nearest thing to hand, which happened to be a headful of hair. I grabbed something else, pulled again. I think I was bellowing, "get the hell off of her," but maybe I was making the same noises as Tora.

Then it was over. The five of them were running. I was watching them dash for the pines with the buttock-roll imposed by their broad pelvises. It looked more like a high-speed waddle than a run. Sometimes it made me laugh aloud. Right then, I didn't think I'd ever find anything funny again.

Tora was crouching over Pilun, running her hands over her head and throat. I looked down, waiting for her small, deft and completely steady hands to answer the question I feared I already knew the answer to. My own hands were shaking so much that I jammed them under my armpits, which only sent the shiver coursing through my torso.

I was about as useful as a dead tree as I looked down on the golden dome of Tora's head and the bloody upheaval of Pilun's. I didn't have Tora's medical training but I didn't need it. When Tora looked up to tell me Pilun was dead, she saw in my face that I already knew.

I closed my eyes. It didn't make it all go away.

Instead, I heard the hum of a drone I hadn't registered while I was looking down. It was hovering at my eye level, which told me someone from the project had taken it over from the AI. The camera was trained on my face, which felt like an accusation.

"If you got any smart ideas, now would be a dope time to mention them," I said.

Whoever was controlling it took the hint and backed it off.

Tora closed Pilun's eyelids. They opened again.

She closed them again, and again they eased open.

"That always works in the movies." Tora didn't take her eyes off Pilun. "I've only seen people die in hospitals. I'd leave the nurses to look after them."

"We should leave her here," I said. "See what they do."

"Yes. We should observe. And interpret."

Tora stood and looked me in the eye with an expression that said, *the hell with observing and interpreting*.

"Yeah." I bent down and scooped Pilun into my arms.

I carried her back to the building and into the mortuary we'd never used. Tora pulled out one of the drawers and I laid Pilun in it. Tora switched on the refrigeration unit while I looked down at Pilun, thinking of the girl I'd watched grow up over the three years since

I'd joined the project. Thinking of how quickly she'd been reduced to the wreckage in front of me.

Over a damn *song*.

Thinking of how thirteen short years of life were reduced to a specimen that would be dissected, photographed and published and presented around the world starting as soon as the Denisovan project truck arrived from Portland.

"It's not right," I said.

I got this job because the project needs someone who knows his way around child and adolescent psychology, not because I was good at profound statements. I didn't take my gaze away from Pilun, but I heard Tora leave the room and come back in. Her hands appeared beside Pilun's head, holding a pair of scissors that she used to cut a lock of Pilun's hair.

"Let's go," she said.

She slid the drawer closed and led me outside, carrying the hair in one hand and a tablet in the other. One of us had thought to worry about what the rest of the Denisovans were doing. The AI had the drone watching over them, huddled together and looking shocked. They had their loin cloths on, which I took to be a good sign.

I followed Tora out of the building and into the forest. She scooped away handfuls of browned pine needles and dug into the mulch with her fingers, releasing the scent of forest soil. She placed Pilun's hair in the dip she'd made and covered it.

Tora's medical background had given her a lot more experience of coping with death than I had. Enough to know that ritual helps to cope with traumatic events, even if the ritual is improvised. I found a few stones and piled them on top of where Pilun's hair lay.

A drone hovered within a few feet as we did it. I presumed everyone else on the project knew what was going on by now, and were holding their own vigil in front of screens showing the feed from that drone's camera.

I placed the last stone I could find and stood beside Tora over the substitute grave.

"You want to say a prayer or something?" she asked.

I thought about that. "No."

"Good."

We joined hands and stood there. Tora's hand felt very small and delicate in my clumsy paw. It felt wrong that holding it felt so good with Pilun chilling in the fridge, but feeling wrong never stopped a damn thing from feeling good.

It didn't feel good when she took her hand away.

"I am going to take a shower, Stanley," she said. "Then we must talk about this."

"Yeah."

I stood alone for a few minutes, then went to get a shower myself.

My room seemed very small when I closed the door. A bed, a chair, a desk with a screen. A box that shut me in with thoughts I'd rather leave outside. Thoughts of the sound of stone on Denisovan skull. Thoughts of five children who had become adolescents who had become murderers and were now — doing what, exactly?

I tapped the screen. It showed the three boys asleep in one of the shelters they'd made and the two remaining girls in the other. They'd taken to separating sleepspace by gender in the last few months, which we took as another reaction to puberty. Late evening was an unusual time for them to be asleep, but then it was hardly a normal day.

In a few minutes, the cameras would switch to infra-red and the contours of their faces would be replaced with the ghostly shades of night vision but there was just enough light left to see them look as peaceful as they always did when they slept. Sometimes I'd watch them like I'd once watched over my own kids, feeling warmed by the sight of a child who felt the world was a safe enough place to sleep in.

The warmth was still there. They were the same boys and girls I'd known since I joined the project three years ago. Yet that warmth now came with the knowledge of what they'd done and what they might do again. We called Denisovans human. The project's geneticists had never agreed on whether they were a different species to us or merely a sub-species but either way, they'd made the word *human* a lot fuzzier around the edges than it used to be.

I knew where I was with sapiens kids. I'd spent fifteen years working with some of the most troubled of them before I joined the Denisovan project. I'd been thinking that kids with no concept of freebasing or gang colors were much easier to understand but now I knew how wrong it was possible to be.

A shower could wait. I told the screen to make a call. It rang for long enough that I was about to give up when my ex-wife said, "Hey Stanley."

The guarded tone and the time it had taken her to answer told me she'd been discussing whether to answer at all with steady-job-in-a-bank new husband, which meant he was in the room with her.

"Hey, Laurel. How're you doing?"

"I'm good. What do you want?"

She was only that blunt when steady-job-in-a-bank new husband was around.

"I'd like to talk to the kids, please, Laurel. Just for a minute."

"Are you drunk?"

I made myself pause before I answered. I'd called because talking to the kids would make me feel more human — in the sense of the word that I'd grown up with — than I did right now. I hadn't called to let Laurel needle me. "No, Laurel, I'm not drunk. I'm in the middle of a pine forest with nothing stronger than soda within five hours' drive. Now can I speak to the kids?"

"They're out. Mitch took them to see *The Aristocats*."

"What, that old cartoon's showing in a theater?"

"No, the new live action one. You know, with the songs."

I didn't know anything about the songs, but I did know that when you lie to a clinical psychologist, you don't give him an obvious tell like throwing in extraneous details. "Please, Laurel. Just for a minute."

"They're at a difficult age, Stanley." The edge in Laurel's voice told me she was pissed that I didn't believe her, especially as she was lying. "You can't just hide in that forest with your Neanderthals and log on to your own kids when it's convenient. I said Mitch took them to the theater and they're in the theater, okay?"

"They're Denisovans. Not Neanderthals."

"Whatever."

I pulled myself up before I got drawn into an argument over what sort of human I was working with. She was calling them Neanderthals for the same reason I refused to use steady-job-in-a-bank new husband's name.

I was about ten seconds away from pointing out that I hadn't joined the Denisovan project until after she'd moved halfway across the country and taken the kids with her, which would provoke her to point out how much I'd been drinking at the time and then we'd be away on the same argument we'd had a hundred times. By the time one of us hung up, we'd have rolled back a year of being able to talk to each other like adults.

"Will you tell them I called?" I said. "Can you please do that?"

"Yes. Yes, okay, Stanley. I'll do that."

"Thank you," I said because she sounded like she meant it.

I must have spent longer deciding to make that call than I'd thought, or perhaps longer staring at the wall afterward, because Tora knocked on my door before I'd made it to the shower.

She was fresh from her own shower in clean jeans and a T-shirt with the Johns Hopkins logo across it, which made me feel even more disheveled than usual. I hoped there were no pine needles in the beard I'd grown to cover my double chins.

For a moment, I thought she was going to come into my room. Of course she didn't. That was no more than the wishful thinking of a man on the brink of middle age who had just failed to fulfill a need for sapiens contact.

I followed her into the kitchen between our rooms where I saw the bottle of Jack Daniels on the formica table.

"I was saving it for the day we finished the rotation. But I need it more now than I will then. I always needed a drink after I lost a patient, and I guess this is the same thing."

She'd already opened the bottle and now she poured two tumblers. "You must need one as much as I do."

She was wrong about that. I craved a drink. I longed for a drink. Which was why a drink was the last thing I needed. One of the attractions of working for the Denisovan project had been the eight-week rotations on a dry site. I was still thinking about that when I threw down the whiskey she passed me.

Tora's eyebrows shot up in surprise, but she refilled my glass. The sweet burn of whiskey slaked a thirst I'd come so close, so agonizingly close, to forgetting.

For about ten seconds.

Because one drink is never enough. I sat at the table, clenching my hands in my lap, each trying to keep the other from the glass that I hated with as much passion as I desired it.

Tora was saying something. She was saying it from the other side of the whiskey, which was a very long way from where I was. I'd never told her about my alcoholism. She had no idea of the bombshell she'd just lobbed at me.

"Stanley? Are you okay?"

"Will you please put the whiskey away?" Speaking those words felt like tearing them from my soul.

Bless Tora. She took one look at my face and put the bottle back in the cabinet. Then she emptied the glasses down the sink.

"I'm sorry, Stanley. I didn't know."

"I'm sorry I didn't tell you." I closed my eyes and tried to pull myself together. "But we need to decide what to do about — about Pilun."

"If you're okay?"

"I'm okay." Sure I was okay. I'd watched a girl being battered to death and I'd fallen off the wagon, and it wasn't even night yet. "Have you heard from anyone else in the project?"

"Yes, I spoke to them. They requested our recommendations." Tora slumped into the chair across the table from me. Her body language said that it was a bad time for me to go to pieces. "No one seems to know what to do."

She'd found time to check in as well as have a shower while I was arguing with Laurel and staring at the wall.

"I was hoping they'd give us some recommendations, not ask for them," I said.

"You're the child psychologist on the ground. I guess they want you to take the lead."

"Me?" It was all I could do not to leap for that cabinet and swig whiskey from the bottle. "What do you think? What happened today?"

"I think it was a game that got out of hand. They've never tried anything like that before. They didn't understand it would kill her. Did you see them sitting together afterward? They're traumatized. They won't do it again."

I added finding the time to consider what had happened and form a hypothesis to the list of things Tora had done. I got up and filled the kettle. It gave me something to do with my hands while I tried to think like a psychologist. It must have helped because I started to see the gap in her thinking.

"I don't think it was a game. It looked like a ritual to me. They were naked. They sat in a precise pattern. And Pilun looked scared, meaning she knew what was about to happen. I think they knew exactly what they were about. Maybe they didn't know how they knew, but they knew."

Tora frowned. "How can it be a ritual, Stanley? They've had no one to teach it to them."

"No, but ... forbidden experiment."

I let that hang in the air. Tora knew about the forbidden experiment as well as I did: you let a bunch of kids grow up without adult supervision and then you find out what innate human behavior looks like because they've never had a culture to learn it from. It's called forbidden because if you were sick enough to do try it with sapiens children, you'd find yourself in jail long before you got any usable results.

Making the forbidden experiment less forbidden had taken one set of geniuses to invent an artificial uterus that they didn't want to test with sapiens babies and another set of geniuses to suggest testing it by resurrecting Denisovans from DNA recovered from the Siberian permafrost.

That was before I joined the project, but I'd noticed that none of the reports used the word 'human' to encompass the Denisovans until after they were born. I guess that's how all those geniuses had been able to see them as a way to square an ethical circle rather than as an ethical dilemma in themselves.

What no set of geniuses had worked out was what six Denisovans who'd died between forty and seventy thousand years ago might have taught their clones if they'd known they were posthumous parents.

At the time, NBC had given the debate between treating the Denisovans as regular sapiens kids and treating them as an uncontacted tribe the occasional snippet, usually between the baseball scores and some senator I'd never heard of talking about the trade deficit. I'd been caught up in trying to keep sapiens kids out of gangs and failing to save my marriage, so I hadn't paid the attention I would have if I'd known I'd be asking the Denisovan project for a job a few years later.

The latter view won out, so the Denisovans got gender-neutral names from an old novel, sapiens wet nurses who were switched often enough to keep them from bonding and a fenced-off chunk of the Pacific Northwest to roam around in. By the time my marriage and sobriety collapsed — I'm still not sure in what order — and I joined the project, they were old enough to do a lot of roaming.

It had gone pretty well up to a couple of hours ago.

"Are you going to make the coffee or not, Stanley?" asked Tora.

"You want some?"

"No."

I touched the kettle. It had boiled while I was thinking about how we'd got here instead of where we should go next.

"Me either." I poured glasses of water for Tora and me and sat back down.

"Then why did you boil the kettle?"

"The same reason you're asking me about it. To distract myself."

It had worked for me. My focus was coming back.

"I don't buy it." Tora was looking at her hands. "You're saying that what happened today was somehow genetically coded? That's a very specific behavior pattern."

"Lots of animals have genetically coded behavior. No mammal mother needs to be told she needs to suckle her young. We don't know what else is in our genes because we all grow up with parents, and in a society. Maybe society's the only thing stopping us going all *Lord of the Flies* on each other."

Tora was still looking down. She didn't like the idea. Neither did I, but that didn't make me wrong.

"You were a trauma surgeon, right?" I asked.

"Right."

"Then you've seen what happens. Kids stabbed or shot by other kids. That kind of thing."

"Sure. It happens. Even sometimes in Stockholm. I saw it a lot more when I moved to Baltimore. But that's because of society. Or because society failed those kids. If it was genetic, it would be the same all over the world. People are ..." She corrected herself. "Sapiens are sapiens. We're not a genetically diverse species. The difference between Stockholm and Baltimore is cultural, not genetic."

I couldn't argue with that. There was more genetic diversity between the five surviving Denisovans than between ten billion living sapiens.

I was still mulling that over while Tora drove home the point. "My son doesn't go around hurting people. Neither do most kids."

"Maybe that just proves your son's got a good mom. I spent years with the kids who don't have a good anyone. Not many things scare me more than a nine-year-old with a switchblade."

"So what should we do? In your opinion?"

I took a deep breath. My opinion was based on what I'd just said. Tora hadn't liked what I'd just said, so she wasn't going to like my opinion. No one in the Denisovan project was going to like my opinion, which meant I'd need Tora on my side when I put it to them.

"End the experiment," I said. "Quit this two-sapiens-at-a-time-while-they-find-their-own-way system and bring in a bunch of us. Denisovans probably grew up in a band. Let's give them a band."

"And teach them to be sapiens instead of Denisovans?" Tora didn't like the idea any more than I'd expected her to. "Or what sapiens think Denisovans might have been?"

"Sure. Why not?"

The hard line of Tora's mouth told me I needed some damn good reasons why not.

"If being Denisovan means killing each other for failing an endurance test," I said, "I'll take a societally corrupted sapiens upbringing for them any day."

"You think it was an endurance test?"

"It's the only explanation I can think of." I wasn't sure where the idea had come from, but it didn't sound crazy so it made as much sense as anything that day. "Singing burns a lot of energy. It was when Pilun couldn't keep up that they turned on her."

"So they killed her for singing a bad note? I can't believe that, Stanley."

"I'd been wrong to think Tora would dislike the idea. She loathed it."

"Okay. What do you think happened?"

"Like I said. A game gone wrong. They got carried away. They didn't even know about death. Now they've seen it, they'll learn from it."

"Sure they know about death. They kill deer, don't they?" I snorted with something too bitter to be called a laugh. "We counted it as a success when they started doing that."

"Sure, but they know the difference between a human and a deer. What they didn't know was that humans are similar enough to be killed like a deer." She looked up. Looked me dead in the eye. "Stanley, Denisovans are so close to sapiens ... if it's in their genes, it's in ours. Yours, mine, my son, your kids. Can you really believe that?"

"Can I believe we have genes that code for our own destruction?" I looked away from Tora's blue-eyed interrogation and found myself looking at the cabinet with the whiskey bottle. "Sure I can."

Tora must have seen where I was looking because she said, "We're talking about genes for violence against each other, not self-destruction."

Ow. I'd asked for that, but it still hurt. I closed my eyes and thought about Tora's question. The truth was that yes, I could believe that the violence I'd seen today was coded in our genes. I wasn't certain of it, but I could believe it more easily than I could dismiss it. What I couldn't do was think of a way to persuade Tora. Not in the face of her naked need to believe that what she'd seen today wasn't human nature set free.

"All right," I said. "Let's do this: no direct intervention right now, but one of us awake at all times watching them. If they even look like they're about to sit in a circle, we buzz them with the drones to distract them until we can get there with the tasers. One more sign of violence, that's the end of the experiment. Can you live with that?"

Tora nodded. "Yes, that's a good plan. I'm sure we won't need to do it, but it's good to be ready."

"Let's do that, then."

I didn't think it was a good plan, but we'd just established that I had a darker view of human nature than Tora's and if we were both reacting to our experiences, how could I tell who was right? No one else in the project was chipping in, let alone offering to judge. In the absence of data, even our scientific geniuses had to fall back on experience.

"Can you tell the project what we decided?" she asked. "I expect they'll be happy someone made a decision. I need to have a long talk with my husband."

"I thought he was on vacation in Australia. What time is it there?"

"I think four in the morning." Tora shrugged. "I'll wake him up. Call me if someone in the project has a different idea but ... after today, I need to hear my husband's voice."

"Sure. Goodnight."

She left me feeling more alone than I had any right to feel. What did I expect? That she was going to forget all about her husband — who she didn't doubt would be delighted to wake up in the small hours of the morning when he heard from her — and fall into my pudgy arms? I'd explained that wasn't how life worked to enough hormone-saturated teenagers that I should have gotten the message myself by now.

Feeling alone was nothing new. I had my ways of coping and if one of those ways was guaranteed to leave me feeling even more alone and with an even bigger problem, it didn't stop me staring at the cabinet door it was sitting behind. If I stared for much longer, I was going to hear Jack Daniels singing to me.

What I needed to do was to call into the project. To get immersed in a conversation between scientists spread across four continents who would have called us by now if they had any idea of what to do. To endure at least two hours of maybes and perhapses before they acknowledged that, imperfect as the plan Tora and I had agreed on, it was the best anyone could come up with right now.

Just thinking about it made me want to hide in the forest. Or crawl under my duvet. Or … screw it. I wasn't kidding myself and it wasn't like there was anyone else around to kid. I'd already had one drink this evening, so one more wouldn't make any difference and it might make that conversation a little more bearable.

Tora was an angel. She'd even left the glasses handy by the sink.

I woke up at the kitchen table with my head in my arms, the smell of bacon and eggs in my nostrils and a forest fire worthy of Southern California blazing in my skull.

"Hi, Stanley," said Tora and placed a fried breakfast in front of me with a clang like the Liberty Bell cracking all over again.

I wanted to bury my head in my hands. I could avoid looking at Tora if I did that. I didn't know how I'd ever look at her again.

She sat across the table from me so I had to look down at the plate, which was a mistake because it made me notice that my stomach was in as sorry a state as my head.

"Stanley, I'm sorry," she said. "I shouldn't have brought the whiskey. I thought … well, I told you why I brought it. It was wrong. This is supposed to be a dry site and I should have followed the rules."

Just when I'd thought I couldn't feel any smaller, she was apologizing to me.

"My fault," I said.

Tora gave me a quizzical look because it had come out, 'muffa.'

It was only then that I noticed the cup of coffee and the packet of Tylenol beside the food. She must have put them there before I woke up. She really was an angel.

"Eat the food, Stanley."

If that was a forest fire in my head, it must have been the fire service helicopter's rotor spinning in my gut.

"It will make you feel better." Tora shrugged. "Trust a doctor to know about hangovers."

My hands were shaking so much I could hardly hold the knife and fork, but I managed to carve off a sliver of egg. I considered eating it.

Wasn't going to happen.

Tora placed a packet of ibuprofen next to the Tylenol. I nodded my thanks and swallowed a couple.

It must have done something because by the time the coffee had cooled enough to sip, I felt a little better. Well enough to look around and see an empty whiskey bottle beside the sink and silently cuss myself out for thinking it was a priority when I didn't know if I'd emptied it myself or whether Tora had poured what I'd left down the sink. Not well enough to put that egg in my mouth.

"Tora, I'm sorry."

It must have come out as recognizable words this time because she waved my apology away. "It was my fault. I didn't know ..."

She left the rest of the sentence unsaid.

"It wasn't your fault. It was my nature."

That must have reminded her of last night's conversation because she glanced at the tablet she'd left on the table. She frowned.

"Stanley, they are naked and they are walking in single file. I think we should be there."

"Uh, yeah." Now I was looking for them, I could see the dark lines under her eyes from spending all night watching over the Denisovans while I was passed out. "I gotta piss."

Tora was on her feet, throwing on her jacket. "I will meet you there. I'm sure it will be fine, but we had better be sure."

She was out of the door before I could remind her to take the taser or any other equipment we had locked away. A couple of minutes before, I wasn't sure I'd ever be able to stand up again but now adrenaline got me to my feet. I grabbed a taser when I'd pissed, thrown on a jacket and scalded my tongue on a mouthful of coffee.

I stumbled out of the door feeling I'd doubled my weight and a flock of bubbles had taken to floating in front of my eyes.

It's easy to get lost in a pine forest. The branches interlock from hip height up to a hundred feet above you, capturing so much light that they hold you in a twilight of their own making on even the brightest day. You can push your way into the forest easily enough, but the branches spring back into place behind you so that after a few paces, all directions look the same in a world of identical trunks and branches.

I was using the GPS on my phone to follow Tora, but neither of us ever left the building without an old-fashioned magnetic compass. A year ago, one of the other guys had forgotten his and dropped his phone into a stream. The waterproof casing leaked and his phone fritzed, and he'd spent the next three hours walking in circles before his partner missed him and used the AI to find him with the drones.

This morning, I didn't have three minutes to spare, let alone three hours. The prick of pine needles on my fingers as I pushed my way into the forest was like pushing my way back into the Pleistocene, when sapiens like me were the newcomers in lands that had long been dominated by natives with paler skins, broader noses and a physiology that let them go naked in a place that would reduce me or my ancestors to shivering uselessness without several layers of garments.

It was only when I caught up to Tora, squatting at the edge of the same clearing that Pilun had died in, that I realized the haze wasn't all in my head. There was a mist lying over the forest, reducing the five Denisovans to silhouettes against the faint, jagged backdrop of pines across the clearing.

Tora nodded to me as I squatted beside her, my breath thundering in my ears as the sweat chilled on my neck. I gave up on the crouch and dropped to a kneel. The Denisovans were already singing. Their beautiful, ethereal, terrible harmony was already gathering pace.

"We need ... to stop ... this now," I panted. "I'll call the project ... they can use the drones ..."

"No, Stanley. They won't kill again."

"You can't know that."

"Stanley, if you call the project, you will be making them into us. You'll take away their chance to be real Denisovans."

I stood up, feeling like I needed a lever to get my knees to straighten. Five Denisovans became ten and the forest floated around me. I staggered against the nearest pine, letting the embrace of its branches hold me up. "Damn it."

Tora stood and faced me. Standing was much easier for her. "They won't hurt each other. Trust me."

Her voice carried an absolute conviction. Her face showed she wasn't seeing the same in my face. "Stay here. I'll show you."

"What do you ...?"

But she was already walking into the clearing. If my head had been clear, I'd have recognized her conviction for what it was: everything she believed about humanity depended on her being right. If she was wrong, it meant that Denisovan violence was etched in their genes and if it was etched in theirs, it was etched in hers.

My head wasn't clear. I was still getting over a headrush that left me unsure which way was up, let alone of my interpretation of Denisovan behavior. When Tora sounded sure and told me to trust her, I was a lot more ready to trust her judgement than mine. I stayed where I was and trusted her as the mist leached the blue from her jacket.

The Denisovans shuffled apart to make a space for her, recreating their hexagon of yesterday.

I rubbed my eyes and stepped away from the tree. My head had stopped swimming, which was a start.

They were alternating. I couldn't tell them apart in the mist, but I could hear the tenor of one of the boys, the alto of one of the girls, a deeper bass, a soprano, another tenor that faded to silence.

No one picked it up.

The silence hit me like an electric shock. Terror cleared the fog from my brain and set me sprinting forward.

Tora tried to pick up the song. Her thin, sapiens torso produced a note that sounded both shrill and reedy after the deep-chested resonance of the Denisovans.

I was fifty paces away. It might as well have been fifty thousand years.

They were on her before she ran out of breath. I was yelling, screaming something as six human silhouettes merged into one mass of amorphous violence.

I had my taser out and as soon as I was close enough to see individual bodies, I fired it. Someone let out a wail and writhed on the ground. I seized arms, yanked hair, grabbed whatever I could get hold of. Tried to burrow my way through them to Tora.

Then they ran. Just as they'd run the day before.

They left Tora's broken body on the ground. Her sightless eyes stared up at me.

Where were you? they demanded. *Why did you trust me?*

A whimper spun me around. Sabul was still there, huddled on the ground with the taser bolts embedded in his back.

"What are you crying about, you pussy?" I kicked him in the ribs. "She's *dead!*"

Sabul shrank away from me, looking up at me with shocked eyes. If he got up and started swinging, he'd have killed me, but to him, I was one of the benign figures who had been in his life for as long as he remembered, only intervening when he or one of his fellows was sick.

Tora lay dead behind me, so I kicked him again.

Sabul was curled into a ball, so my next kick caught him on the back.

Tora would tell me I was kicking a child. The Denisovan skeleton was strong enough that I'd do more damage by kicking a pine trunk, but I knew enough about kids to know how devastating it was when a benign presence in their life becomes a source of pain.

I still wanted to kick him again.

Instead, I dropped to my knees and roared out every cubic inch of air in my lungs. It left me gasping for breath. Or perhaps I was sobbing.

A sound like a wail, but an octave lower, pulled my head out of my hands to see Sabul's twisted face. Electric shocks and booted kicks were new experiences for him. He was terrified of what might be next.

Except that when the other Denisovans didn't want to be hurt, they'd run away.

The truth forced its way through the rage and grief flooding my mind. Sabul didn't expect me to hurt him. Sabul expected me to kill him.

A lot of kids have looked at me like I was their enemy. It goes with the job. None had ever expected me to kill them before.

I felt hungover all over again.

Sabul didn't look like he felt it when I pulled the taser bolts out.

"I won't hurt you," I said.

He might not understand the words, but at least he'd hear I wasn't singing.

I crouched in front of Sabul and took hold of his wrists. He let me pull him to his feet. I stood back and he jogged in the direction the others had run. He threw a look over his shoulder, which might have meant he was afraid I was chasing him or just that he was trying to make sense of me.

I looked down at Tora. "What would you do?"

He blue eyes still looked so full of life. They dared me to know how she'd answer.

I scooped her up and carried her into the mortuary. She was lighter than Pilun had been, which felt wrong. She should have been heavy enough to justify the weight I carried in my stomach.

I put her in the mortuary drawer. I should have undressed her, but I wasn't equal to that.

"What would you do?"

The drawer was level with my waist, so she was able to look back and tell me I knew the answer.

Which I did, even if I didn't have long to act on it. If no one from the project team had called me, it was because they were waiting for me to call them. That didn't mean they would be doing nothing. There would already be a truck on its way from Portland.

It was about five seconds after I pulled the plug on the server controlling the drones that my phone rang. I let it ring. The only answer I could give to the inevitable "what the hell are you doing?" was "what Tora would have wanted." They wouldn't understand that. They'd try to talk me out of it, and they might have succeeded.

I switched my phone to silent so I could use the GPS but ignore the barrage of incoming calls and texts. I filled a rucksack with nutrient bars, a pair of pliers and a roll of duct tape. I threw in a couple of pints of water for myself and Tora's Tylenol and ibuprofen, which I was feeling the need for now that the adrenaline was wearing off.

I followed the GPS to find the place where the Denisovans slept. The five of them were sitting between the boys' and the girls' sleepspaces, holding hands and looking like children trying to make sense of a world that they'd just discovered didn't work the way they thought it did.

I took the battery out of my phone, rendering myself invisible to the rest of the project and anyone else except the Denisovans.

The five of them were watching me in silence. I pulled out a nutrient bar and crouched a few paces in front of Sabul. He watched me for a few moments, like a sapiens kid being offered his favorite candy by a stranger. His recent lesson in stranger danger wasn't strong enough to overcome temptation so he shuffled over and took it. He had a graze on his flank from my boot, but it didn't look like it was bothering him any.

The other four were watching me now, so I gave them a bar each. They were as chronically hungry as active kids everywhere, and I'd only given them enough to whet their appetites.

Some of their spears were lying around so I scooped a couple of them under my arm. They'd need those.

I took Sabul's hand in one of mine and started walking. The other four followed so I risked letting go of Beshun to get my magnetic compass out of my jacket pocket.

We walked for hours, following the compass eastward. If the Denisovans showed signs of flagging interest, I passed around more food. I didn't have to worry about them getting tired. They could walk for much longer than I could. I didn't know if I'd ever walked fifteen miles before, and if I did, I hadn't been bashing my way through pine branches on a morning after I'd drunk myself into a stupor, and I hadn't been carrying spears that caught on every other branch I tried to push out of my way.

By the time we reached the fence, I was ready to collapse. The Denisovans kept a safe distance from it, even after I'd cut the wires. I had to clamber through with another food bar each.

I put down the spears and gave Sabul the rucksack, showing him how to put it on. He looked doubtful.

"Take it," I said. "It's the last you'll get from me."

I clambered back through the fence and duct taped the wires back in place. It wouldn't restore the current, but none of them looked tempted to test it. I walked along the fence for a while. They followed me from the other side of it.

"Quit following me. You're on your own now."

Five uncomprehending Denisovans looked back at me.

"If we're gonna do the forbidden experiment, we're gonna do it properly. Scram."

I turned my back and walked back into the forest until there were enough branches in the way that we couldn't see each other. Or perhaps until I couldn't walk another step. I sat down with my back to a tree. I must have dozed because I opened my eyes to find dusk darkening the forest.

I retraced my footprints to the fence and saw five sets of wide-toed footprints heading away from the fence, into the forest on the other side.

There's a hell of a lot of pine forest in the Pacific Northwest. More than enough for five Denisovans to hide in.

I put the battery back in my phone and waited to be found.

When anyone asks me, I say I think they'll kill each other out there. I think it's in their nature as much as it's in ours, but we don't know how to moderate their impulses like we do our own kids'. If I'm right, that's the logical conclusion to the forbidden experiment and a damn good reason why it should stay forbidden.

If Tora was right, they'll find a way to live with each other, to survive, maybe make little Denisovans. We'll meet them again, or some sapiens will, when there are enough of them to make a culture of their own.

I like Tora being right better.

Good luck, boys and girls.

ABOUT THE AUTHOR

DJ Cockburn funded his unfortunate writing habit through medical research on various parts of the African continent and drinking a lot of coffee. Earlier phases of his life have included teaching unfortunate children and experimenting on unfortunate fish.

In between a steady drizzle of rejections, he's seen a few stories in venues including *Apex*, *Interzone,* and Gardner Dozois's *Year's Best Science Fiction* for 2014.

His website is at *cockburndj.wordpress.com* and he has occasionally been caught twittering as *@DJ_Cockburn*.

YOU MIGHT ALSO ENJOY

HOT DROP
by J Dark

What starts as a rescue mission in a combat zone on a hostile planet becomes something more.

LITTLE GREEN MEN
by Curtis Bass

The landing of the first manned missions to Mar is perfect until one crew member claims they are being watched by indigenous creatures.

SONGS OF A DEAD FOREST
by Travis Wade Beaty

Old songs can bring new life.

Available in digital and trade paperback editions from
Water Dragon Publishing
waterdragonpublishing.com

www.ingramcontent.com/pod-product-compliance
Lightning Source LLC
Chambersburg PA
CBHW030826200726
48288CB00004B/1423